Corky's
PET PARADE

Written & Illustrated by MAGGI FIEDLER

PIED PIPER BOOKS : *NEW YORK*

DESIGNED AND PRODUCED BY THE DOMESDAY PRESS, INC.

MANUFACTURED IN THE U.S.A.

COPYRIGHT 1946, BY PIED PIPER BOOKS, INC.

BINDING BY F. M. CHARLTON CO., INC.

Corky gaily waved good-bye to his mother and
sisters as he started off for the park.

He was very pleased with himself for here he
was going off alone for a whole day of play. Of
course he did feel a little sad about having to leave
his pet chicken at home, but his mother had given
strict orders that Beulah was to stay in the yard
with the other chickens. So with one last look at
Beulah, he went happily on his way.

Corky's mother had prepared a good-sized lunch for him and put it all in a brown paper bag. When he reached the park, he was already beginning to feel small rumblings in his stomach so, without any further delay, he sat down on a park bench and ate all the lunch.

He peeled the last banana and ran eagerly to the top of a small hill in the park. There below him in a beautiful sunny space was the playground!

"Oh boy!" he thought, "This will be lots of fun."

With a happy sigh he trotted down the hill to the wonderland below.

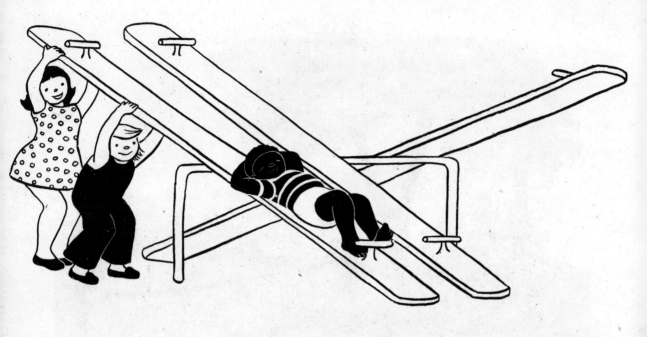

As soon as he arrived he headed for the see-saw. Here was something he had always wanted to do, but he had no one to see-saw with, so he plopped down on the board and dozed off. Two small girls stood watching the sleeping Corky and immediately decided to play a trick on him. The biggest girl went to the other side of the see-saw and pulled it down as best she could, almost to the ground.

Corky and the see-saw bounced to the other end with a great crash! The two mischief-makers laughed and giggled at the sight of Corky with such a surprised look on his face.

"Well," said Corky, as he picked himself up. "That sure wasn't very funny."

But the two rascals only laughed harder. And Corky, still a little dazed at the welcome he had received, strutted off for new fields to conquer.

The first thing he came to was the sand-box.
He sat down and started piling up the sand. Soon
he had almost all the sand in the entire box beside
him and was busily building a huge castle. All the
other children sat watching as the castle grew bigger
and bigger under Corky's quick fingers.

"Oh Boy!"

"My!"

"Gracious!"

"Lookit the size of it."

All the children marveled as Corky modeled away, never noticing that he was the center of attraction.

Suddenly, one of the boys shouted, "Look out, here comes Homer!"

Corky went right on building his castle.

"H-m-mm," he thought to himself, "Guess I'll build a tower on the top."

The next thing he knew, he was lying on the ground. A huge dog was standing above him with his pink tongue hanging out.

"Oh g-g-g-golly!" breathed Corky.

A little girl ran up laughing and yelling, "Come here, Homer you bad dog."

She took him by the collar and pulled him away, saying politely to Corky, who was half covered up with sand, "I'm awfully sorry, but Homer likes sand and whenever he sees it he just runs wild."

With that she dragged Homer away, shaking her head at him and looking at frightened Corky.

For the second time that morning Corky picked himself up. He carefully shook all the sand out of his shirt and hair and ears.

"My goodness, I'm thirsty," he said as he ran his tongue around his mouth, tasting little particles of sand as it went. He took the last few pebbles of sand from between his toes and set out to look for the drinking fountain.

There it was, among the cool trees. No one was drinking at the fountain so Corky ran eagerly to it, watched the water spout from its hole, and thirstily gulped it down. He drank and drank, and a small line of waiting children formed behind him. With a final gulp he let the water squirt over his hot face and trickle down.

"Now I'm going to take it easy and not get in any more trouble." And he sauntered along, whistling as he went.

He was heading for a bench when he heard a small cluck-clucking behind him. There was Beulah, his own chicken, pecking along as though she owned the park!

"Beulah," said Corky, as he pointed an accusing finger at the happy hen, "Mamma told you to stay home."

Beulah just clucked contentedly and blinked innocently at Corky.

"Well, I suppose you'll have to stay. So come on," said Corky, shrugging his shoulders.

She followed him to a big table where a lot of boys and girls were watching a checker game.

"Here's a new boy, Butch," shouted a girl's voice.

Before he realized what was going on, Corky was playing checkers with the champion of the play-ground who was called Butch.

The game was very exciting. Corky knew how to play checkers better than any other game and now he was sure to win. He did.

Everyone was laughing at Butch for it was the first game he had lost all summer. But Butch didn't seem to mind. He and Corky had started an excited

conversation about Beulah.

"Come on, I'll show you!" said Butch.

Corky followed obediently, with Beulah pecking along in the rear.

"See!" said Butch firmly as he pointed to a huge sign hanging from two wooden posts.

"Golly, you're right," Corky replied. "Do you think I could enter Beulah in a big show like that. She's only a chicken, and a funny red one at that."

"Course you can. One time we even had a skunk!"

"All right, I'll enter Beulah." And Corky turned to explain to his chicken, but she wasn't there. She had disappeared!

"Oh, oh," cried Corky, "Beulah's gone and got herself lost. I better find her."

Off went Corky. He looked in trees, behind benches, and even in the brook, shouting for Beulah as he tramped from place to place. He was standing still for a moment to look about him when he heard a soft sound.

"Cluck."

Corky looked up and there was Beulah perched on the trick bar.

"You come down from there, you crazy hen!" said Corky, shaking a big stick at poor Beulah. Beulah looked sad for a moment, ruffled her feathers, and came down.

Corky borrowed a polka-dot ribbon from a fat little girl, and proceeded to tie a bow around his chicken's neck. Beulah occupied herself by looking cross-eyed at a big dog who was busily sniffing at her.

"Come on, you're going to win first prize in the pet show."

He tugged at the string around Beulah's neck and she followed very reluctantly. They came to a clearing and there in a great crowd were all the children with their different pets. There were snakes, parrots, dogs, rabbits, cats, birds, and even fish! As far as Corky could see, Beulah was the only chicken.

Corky stood around with the other children and their fine pets and waited for the show to begin.

But what chance did a common chicken have of winning first prize in the show—very little, indeed!

"Don't worry, Beulah," said Corky. "When the judges see *you* they'll *have* to sit up and take notice!"

The judges were two girls and two boys who sat on a special bench and watched all the pets go by. When the time came for Corky to march Beulah past the judges, she was gone — again! Poor Corky looked frantically about him, but no Beulah. She was really gone this time. He looked to the judges for help—but what was this!!

The three prize winners had already been chosen. A little boy stood proudly next to his huge sleepy dog who had a blue ribbon on his collar. Next to

them were the second and third prize winners. A porcupine, of all things, and a tiny little dog who looked hungry.

One of the judges told all the excited owners of pets that a big silver cup would be given later on to the most accomplished pet.

Corky thought sadly, "Well, Beulah won't win that either, she can't even cluck loud enough."

He wandered over to a grassy space to sit down and almost sat on someone's pet. Why, it was Beulah! Clucking for all she was worth and looking up at Corky with a proud shine in her funny eyes.

At first, Corky did not understand what Beulah was trying to say.

But then he looked down on the grassy spot where Beulah stood and what do you think he saw?

"Wow!" shouted Corky, "Beulah's gone and laid an egg!"

There on the grass lay a beautifully shaped white egg.

All the other children looked in amazement at

the miracle. And all the while Beulah stood there proudly guarding her very first egg.

"Show it to the judges, Corky," said the others.

Corky carefully picked up Beulah's freshly-laid egg and held it in front of him as though it were the most precious jewel in the world.

Then he walked slowly to the judges' stand with Beulah strutting proudly behind him.

When the judges saw Corky coming towards

them with the egg in his outstretched hands they could hardly believe their eyes.

All they could do was stare and stare and stare some more.

Then one of them stood up on the bench and asked Corky, "Did your chicken lay that egg?"

Corky shook his head up and down and so did all the other children.

Yes, Beulah laid the egg.

"Then *he* must be a hen!" cried one of the judges.

"So *he* is!" said another.

They soon decided that Beulah was the most accomplished pet the playground had ever seen and they all agreed to give Beulah the silver cup.

In a voice that everyone could hear, one of the boy judges announced:

"The silver cup prize for the most accomplished pet in the playground goes to Beulah!"

Everyone cheered and clapped as Corky accepted the silver cup from the judges. This was undoubtedly the proudest moment of life for him and for Beulah.

Now at last it was over. Corky and his proud pet trudged wearily to a nearby weeping willow tree and fell fast asleep beneath its shady branches.

When he awoke it was dusk and there before him were his two little sisters with the express wagon.

"Mamma got worried about you, Corky. It's awfully late."

"I guess it is," mumbled Corky sleepily as he plunked himself with great effort into the wagon.

"Why do we always have to come get you?" his sister Susie asked.

But all Corky could reply was "Beulah won the silver cup. She laid an egg!"

"Beulah did?" his sisters exclaimed.

"My, no wonder she looks so pleased."

They both touched the beautiful cup and looked at the egg with amazement.

"C'mon, let's show Mama."

And with that the two little girls tugged at the wagon and started off toward home with Corky and Beulah fast asleep in the express wagon.